ROSEBUD

Babette Douglas

Illustrated by
John Johnson

Productions

Kiss A Me™ Productions, Inc. produces toys and booklets for children with an emphasis on love and learning. For more information on how to purchase a Kiss A Me collectible and plush toy or to receive information on additional Kiss A Me products, write or call:

Kiss a me™ Productions

Kiss A Me Productions, Inc.
90 Garfield Ave.
Sayville, NY 11782
888 - KISSAME
888-547-7263

About the *Kiss a me™* Teacher Creature Series:
This delightfully illustrated series of inspirational books by
Babette Douglas has won praise from parents and educators alike.
Through her wonderful "teacher creatures" she imparts profound lessons of tolerance
and responsible living with heartwarming insights and a humorous touch.

Rosebud

Written by Babette Douglas
Illustrated by John Johnson

ISBN 1-890343-412-9
Printed in China

www.kissame.com

To *Unseen Love.*

This could be a true story.
Who is to know...

One day on a rose
In a bush by the sea,
A small praying mantis
Pondered what prayer might be.

"Although people comment
That praying mantises pray,
I'm really not sure
That's what I'm doing each day.

"So I'll go to the people
That do pray each day
And ask them to teach me
The prayers that they pray."

He then went to a church
That he found near the shore
And kneeled with the people
And waited for more.

"These people are praying.
They are truly in prayer.
Yet, I'm missing the special
Feeling they share."

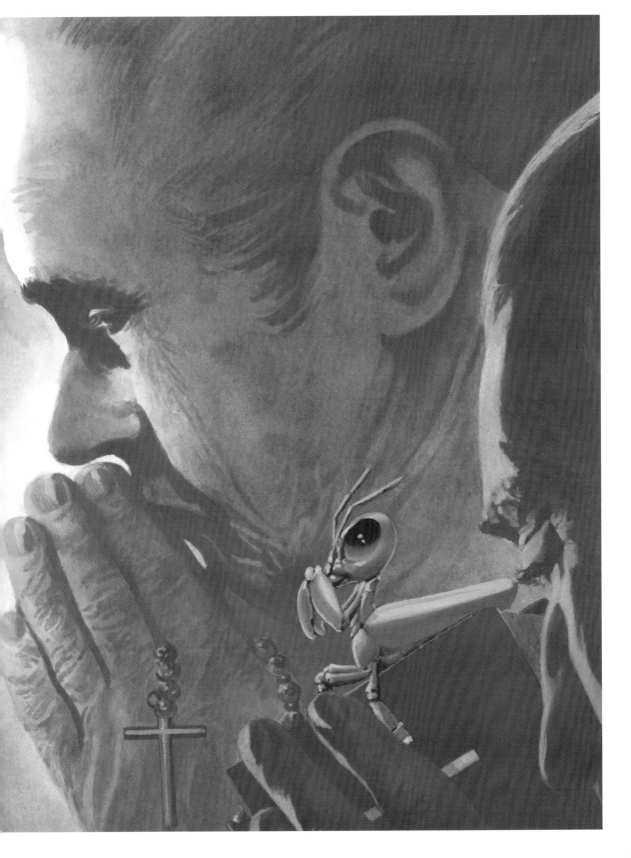

He went from the church
To a mosque far away.
He prayed on the floor
But felt his feelings stray.

He flew to the dervishes
And whirled with the group,
But he just became dizzy,
So out he did troop.

"These people are praying.
They are truly in prayer.
Yet, I'm missing the special
Feelings they share."

"I'll go next to the Indians
On America's shore
And chant with the elders
Who might teach me more."

The Indians chanted
And danced on the ground.
Yet, the little praying mantis
Still searched for what must be found.

"These people are praying.
They are truly in prayer.
Yet, I'm missing the special
Feelings they share."

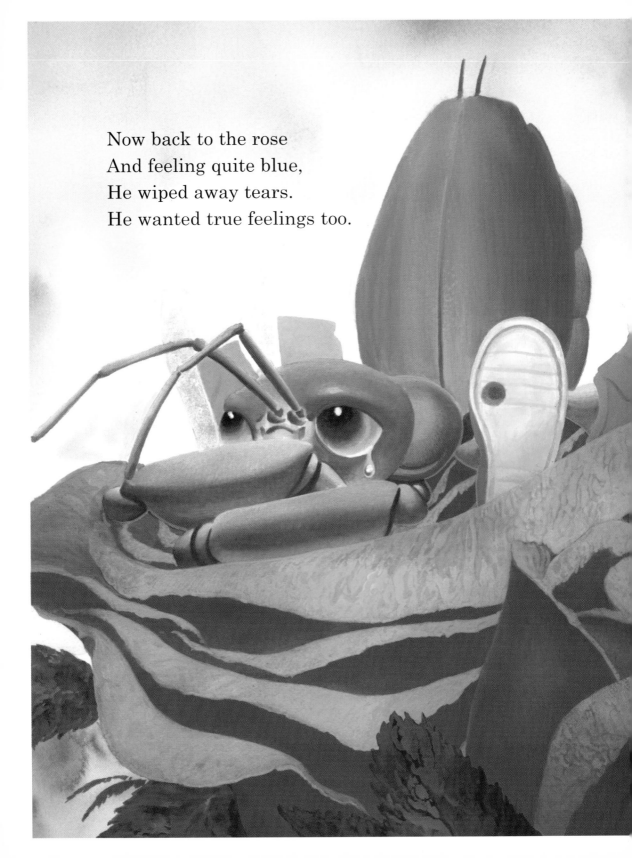

Now back to the rose
And feeling quite blue,
He wiped away tears.
He wanted true feelings too.

"I'm off next to temple,
For the Torah is true.
It might lend some light
On what true feelings do."

And the temple held people
Who prayed every day.
But no one could tell him
Where true feelings lay.

"These people are praying.
They are truly in prayer.
Yet, I'm missing the special
Feelings they share."

The little mantis was weary.
He began to despair.
Where are the true feelings
That turn speech into prayer?

Again, he sat dejected
And stared silent at his toes.
He began to hear a whisper
From deep within the rose.

"Somebody loves you,"
The little rose said.
"Sit quietly for a moment.
Hear with the heart, not with the head.

"Who created the flowers
That grow everywhere,
Bursting with colors,
With fragrance to share?

"Who made the trees
To grow straight and tall,
Shading us in summer,
Dazzling us in fall?

"Who gave us water
To refresh us each day,
To use as a drink
Or for swim and for play?

"Who gave us animals
So we're never alone,
To work with us daily
Or as company at home?

"Whom do we go to
When we're feeling blue?
Who never deserts us
As even friends do?

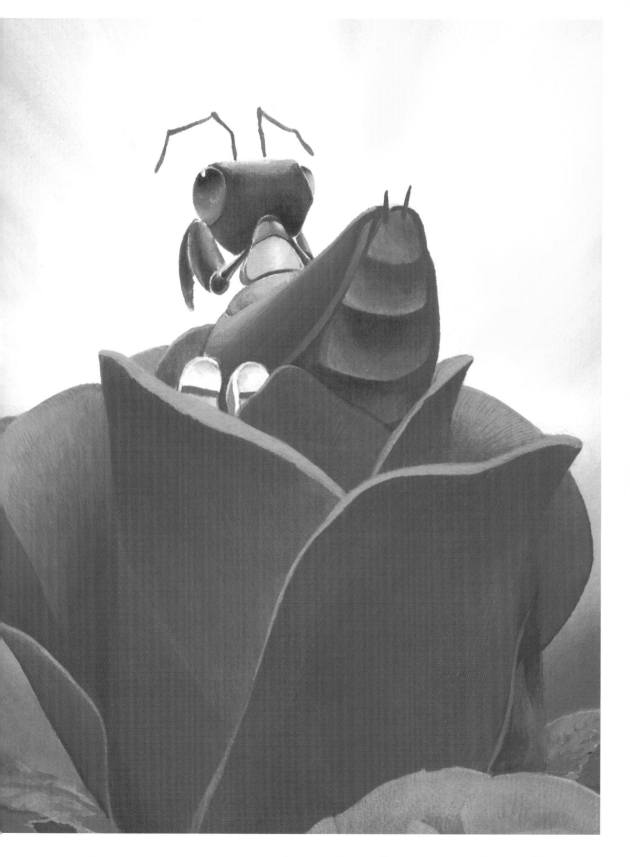

"The feeling most special
Of which you are a part
Is the movement of Love
Right there in your heart."

The little mantis started.
The truth became clear to see.
"Is whoever made the world
The same as who made me?"

"Yes! Unseen Love has created
All that you can view
And made as well the part
That lives on earth as you.

"You're a little praying mantis,
Resting upon a rose.
Yet, even you must feel the love
From which only goodness flows.

"Love gives you true feeling,
A heart that's soaring free!
Now you too feel the Love
Who resides within, with thee.

With love and words together,
Your whispered prayers will soar.
And the Unseen Love who's listening
Will hear those whispers – as a roar."

THE END

Babette Douglas, a talented poet and artist, has written over 30 children's books in which diverse creatures live together in harmony, friendship and respect. She brings to her delightful stories the insights and caring accumulated in a lifetime of varied experiences.

"I believe strongly in the healing power of love," she says. "I want to empower children to see with their hearts and to love all the creatures of the earth, including themselves." The unique stories told by her "teacher creatures" enable children to learn to recognize their own gifts and to value tolerance, compassion, optimism and perseverance.

Ms. Douglas, who was born and educated in New York City, has lived in Sayville, New York for over forty years.

Additional Kiss A Me™ *teacher-creature stories:*

AMAZING GRACE

BLUE WISE

BLUFFALO Wins His Great Race

CURLY HARE™ Gets it Straight

FALCON EDDIE

THE FLUTTERBY

KISS A ME: A Little Whale Watching

KISS A ME Goes to School

KISS A ME To the Rescue

LARKSPUR

THE LYON BEAR™

THE LYON BEAR™ deTails

THE LYON BEAR™: The Mane Event

MISS EVONNE And The Mice of Nice

MISS TEAK And the Endorphins

NOREEN: The Real King of the Jungle

OSCARPUS

SQUIRT : The Magic Cuddle Fish

Character toys are available for each book.
For additional information on books, toys,
and other products visit us at:

www.kissame.com